SPECIAL THANKS TO ANNE MARIE RYAN

ORCHARD BOOKS
Carmelite House
50 Victoria Embankment
London EC4Y 0DZ

First published by Orchard Books in 2018

A CIP catalogue record for this book is available
from the British Library.

ISBN 978 1 40835 216 8

1 3 5 7 9 10 8 6 4 2

Printed in Great Britain

Orchard Books
An imprint of Hachette Children's Group
Part of The Watts Publishing Group Limited
An Hachette UK Company
www.hachette.co.uk

MISSION IMPUFFABLE

ORCHARD

MEET THE POWERPUFF GIRLS!

Favourite colour: Pink
Aura power: Sponge, broom, stapler
Likes: Organising, stationery, science, punching baddies and doing well at school
Dislikes: Mess, being disorganised
Most likely to say: "Let's go save the day!"

Favourite colour: Blue
Likes: Animals, creating computer games, make-up, punching baddies, singing, her toy octopus, Octi
Dislikes: Animals being upset, dressing up in ugly clothes
Most likely to say: "I love piggies!"

Favourite colour: Green
Aura power: Rocket, tank, submarine, cannon
Likes: Roller derby, fighting, deathball
Dislikes: Dressing up, wussy people
Most likely to say: "Don't call me princess!"

THE PROFESSOR: The Powerpuff Girls' father, the Professor, was trying to create the perfect little girls out of sugar and spice and all things nice. But when he accidentally added Chemical X to the mix, he got three super cute and super fierce crime-fighting superheroes: The Powerpuff Girls!
Likes: Science, The Powerpuff Girls, creating new inventions in his lab under the house
Dislikes: When things explode
Most likely to say: "How could you hate science?"

PACK RAT:
This rodent thief loves all things shiny!
Likes: Shiny things
Dislikes: Getting caught
Most likely to say: "Pack Rat is the king of shiny things!"

THE NARRATOR:

Ahem, and there's me. I'm your friendly narrator. I'll pop up now and again to give you all the gossip on what's going on. Are you sitting comfortably? No? Well then, get ready! Honestly, do I have to do everything around here? The book's about to begin! Ready? Then let's go!

CONTENTS

CONTENTS

A RUDE AWAKENING

> *ZZZZZZ! The Powerpuff Girls were sound asleep in their bed. Don't they look peaceful? It would be such a shame to wake them up …*

BRIIINNNGG!

Buttercup's eyes snapped open. She switched off the alarm clock on her bedside table, then flew into the bathroom.

Blossom was still fast asleep. In her dream, she was giving a speech to the United Nations. "And that is how we will achieve world peace," she announced triumphantly. As the audience cheered wildly, another alarm clock rang.

BRIIIIIIIINNNGG!

Blossom sat up in bed and rubbed her eyes. She squinted at the alarm clock. The display said 7:00am.

"That's odd," she said. "I must have set it early by mistake."

She hit the snooze button and went back to sleep.

Next to her, Bubbles was snoring gently and cuddling Octi, her purple stuffed octopus toy.

BRIIIIIIIIIIIIINNNGG!

Another alarm clock started ringing.

"Nooo!" groaned Bubbles. "I haven't had enough beauty sleep." She pulled her pillow over her head to block out the alarm.

"Wakey, wakey!" shouted Buttercup.

SPLASH!

She tipped a bucket of cold water on to her sisters.

"Hey!" squealed Bubbles.

"Yikes!" shrieked Blossom.

Suddenly wide awake, Bubbles and Blossom jumped out of the soggy bed. Their wet pyjamas made puddles on the rug.

"What gives, Buttercup?" said Blossom, glaring at her sister.

"You slept through the first three alarms," she told them. "I needed a back-up plan."

Blossom pushed wet hair out of her face. "Your back-up plan stinks!"

"Hey," said Buttercup. "Don't pour cold water on it. I thought you'd be happy. You're the one who's always saying it's important to have a Plan B!"

Buttercup tossed towels to her shivering sisters. "It didn't just wake you up," she told them. "It also saved time. Now you don't need to take a shower!"

"Why are you in such a hurry this morning?" Bubbles asked. Normally Buttercup had to be dragged out of bed on school days.

"Have you forgotten what today is?" asked Buttercup.

Bubbles thought for a moment. "Is it Unicorn Appreciation Day?"

"Do we have a maths test?" Blossom asked hopefully.

"No," said Buttercup. "It's our school trip to the Townsville Museum!"

"Yay!" said Blossom. "We're going to have so many learning opportunities!"

"What are you talking about?" said Buttercup. "School trips mean no work. Woo hoo!"

"I can't wait to see all the cute animals," said Bubbles. The Townsville Museum had a massive natural history section full of all kinds of dinosaur bones and ancient stuffed animals.

"Dude, you know they're dead, right?" said Buttercup.

"I hope we have time to see everything – there's a huge science exhibition and a fascinating local history display," said Blossom.

"It's going to be awesome!" said Buttercup.

Blossom looked at her sister suspiciously. "I didn't know you were interested in local history, Buttercup."

"I'm not," said Buttercup. "I just can't wait to see Fat Mabel."

"It's not nice to call people rude names," said Bubbles.

"Fat Mabel isn't a person," explained Buttercup. "She's a cannon. One of the most powerful in the world. Now COME ON!"

The Powerpuff Girls got
dressed quickly and went
downstairs to breakfast.
Professor Utonium was stirring
a saucepan of bubbling
porridge. He had
an apron on over his
lab coat.

"You girls are up
early today," said the
Professor.

"We're going to the
Townsville Museum on a
school trip," Buttercup
told him.

"That sounds very
educational," said the
Professor approvingly.

He scooped porridge into their bowls.

"We don't have time for breakfast," said Buttercup. "We're in a rush."

"Growing girls need to eat a well-balanced breakfast," said Professor Utonium. "It's scientifically proven to be the most important meal of the day."

"We get to see the grand unveiling of the Rainbow Heart Tiara today," said Blossom as they sat down. "It belonged to Cleopatra."

The ancient Egyptian queen was one of The Powerpuff Girls' heroes.

"Cleopatra kicked butt," said Buttercup.

"And she had great taste in accessories," said Bubbles.

"Ah yes," said the Professor. "The museum's security is going to be very tight. The tiara is priceless."

Buttercup had already finished a second helping of porridge. "Could you eat any slower?" she asked her sisters. She gobbled up the last few bites of Bubbles's porridge. "Can we go now?"

Professor Utonium opened up his newspaper. The headline read: *Rodent Robber Raids Retailers.*

"Looks like Pack Rat has been stealing jewellery again," said Blossom.

"That reminds me," gasped Bubbles. "I forgot to put on any accessories!"

"We don't have time!" said Buttercup.

"There's always time to accessorise!" replied Bubbles. She flew back upstairs.

When she came back downstairs, she was wearing a sparkly necklace, glittery bracelets and several shiny rings.

"NOW can we go?" said Buttercup impatiently.

"Wait!" cried Blossom. "I need to pack my school supplies!"

Buttercup groaned in frustration. "We're going on a school trip," she said. "You don't need school supplies!"

"I want to take notes on everything we learn at the museum!" said Blossom. She ran upstairs and came back down with a backpack bulging with notebooks, pens and highlighters in every shade of the rainbow.

Finally, The Powerpuff Girls made it out of the door. When they reached the end of the path the front door opened again.

"Girls!" called Professor Utonium. "You forgot your packed lunches!"

Buttercup gasped. She sped down the path and grabbed the lunchboxes. "That would have been a disaster!"

"Be good, girls!" called the Professor as The Powerpuff Girls flew away. "Have fun! Work hard!"

A bus was already waiting outside the school gates when they arrived. The children climbed inside. Bubbles and Buttercup sat next to each other.

"Hey, Blossom!" called a dark-haired boy with glasses. "There's a seat next to me!"

Blossom's cheeks turned as pink as her dress.

"Thanks, Jared," she said, sitting down next to him.

"Blossom and Jared sitting in a tree," sang Buttercup. "K-I-S-S-I-N-G!"

Blossom glared at her sister. "Cut it out, Buttercup!"

The bus started driving to the museum. Before long, though, it came to a halt.

"Come on, come on!" muttered Buttercup. She looked out of the window and

saw a long queue of cars.

HONK HONK!

They were stuck in a traffic jam.

"We're never going to get to the museum at this rate!" groaned Bubbles.

"Oh, yes we are!" said Buttercup. She marched to the front of the bus. "Let me off!" she ordered the driver.

Using her superstrength, Buttercup picked up the bus. Holding it over her head,

she soared up into the sky. She flew to the museum and set the bus down outside.

"We're here!" Buttercup cried. Finally, the school trip could begin!

THE RAINBOW HEART TIARA

Question: What are the two best things about museums?
Answer: The gift shop and the café!

Everyone trooped off the school bus and into the museum. It was a huge white building with steps leading up to an entrance porch with thick pillars. Once inside the

museum, the children
shot off in different
directions, chatting
excitedly.

Blossom studied the floor plan
carefully. "Hmm," she said. "So
many exhibits, so little time."

"Where are the cannons?" Buttercup
asked.

"Can we see the animals first?" asked
Bubbles.

"Are we allowed to go to the gift shop?"
asked Jared.

"Is it time to eat our packed lunches yet?"
asked a boy.

"Where's the toilet?" asked a girl, crossing
her legs and bobbing up and down.

"Attention, children," called Ms Keane,

clapping her hands. Everyone ignored her.

"I've got this," Bubbles told her teacher. "SHUUUUUT UUUUP!!!" she sang in a high, sweet voice. It was so loud that it shattered a glass case holding a collection of prehistoric tin openers. Suddenly, all of the children fell quiet.

"Thanks, Bubbles," said Ms Keane, smiling gratefully. "Now, if you will all follow me, we'll begin our tour."

But they weren't the only ones planning a trip to the museum that morning ...

Deep underneath the Townsville dump, Pack Rat was in his den. The cave was crammed full of shiny things the rat had stolen. There were spoons and forks, bottle tops, trophies – and lots and lots of jewellery!

It glittered in the green glow of toxic waste.

Pack Rat smoothed out a crumpled leaflet with his ring-covered fingers. It was an advertisement for the grand unveiling of the Rainbow Heart Tiara at the Townsville Museum.

"Look, Rita!" Pack Rat said, waving it in front of a plastic baby doll. "Shiny!"

His long tail twitched excitedly as he giggled. "It will be mine!" He put on his yellow jacket and kissed his doll goodbye.

"Pack Rat will bring Baby Rita the shiniest shiny thing of all!"

He scurried off through the slimy sewers below the city. As he headed towards the museum, Pack Rat sang to himself:

"Shiny things, shiny things! Pack Rat is the king of shiny things!"

Meanwhile, back at the museum, The Powerpuff Girls and their classmates were exploring Townsville's most precious artefacts.

They saw a model of the town hall made entirely of ice lolly sticks.

OOOOH!

They admired a handkerchief that the very first mayor of Townsville had used to blow his nose.

AAAAAH!

They saw a display of old coins, a collection of toenail clippings and a prototype for the first ever salad spinner.

"Here we have examples of all of Townsville's creatures," said Ms Keane, leading them into the natural history gallery. There were moth-eaten stuffed squirrels and skunks, pigeons and porcupines, raccoons and rabbits. There was even an enormous chinchillasaurus!

"Aw," said Bubbles. "It's cute!"

"These things give me the creeps," said Buttercup, shuddering.

"I swear that one just moved," said Blossom, pointing to the rodent display.

The next room had dinosaur skeletons in it, including one of an enormous T-Rex.

"He reminds me of Rexy," said Bubbles. Rexy was Bubbles's T-Rex aura.

"Time to move on to another really exciting exhibit," called Ms Keane.

"Finally!" said Buttercup. "We're going to see Fat Mabel!"

Instead, they went into the rocks and minerals room. The display cabinets were filled with lumps in varying shades of grey.

"This is a very special rock," said Ms Keane, stopping in front of a big grey stone.

"It's a rock," muttered Buttercup.

"It is a meteorite from outer space," said Ms Keane. "Can anyone guess what planet it came from?"

"From Uranus?" Buttercup called out.

Her classmates giggled.

Blossom waved her hand in the air.

"Yes, Blossom," said Ms Keane.

"From Mars," said Blossom.

"Correct!" said Ms Keane.

They moved on to the local history exhibition.

"Here are the tools used by the first settlers in Townsville," said the teacher, pointing to a display with a hammer, some rusty tongs and Ye Olde Cordless Drill.

Everyone was starting to look really bored. Well, all except for Blossom. She had already filled one notebook with notes and had started on a second one!

"Is this the way to the cannons?" asked Buttercup as they trooped behind Ms Keane, passing the world's second-largest ball of

elastic bands and a collection of antique pickle jars.

"No, it's lunchtime!" announced Ms Keane as they went into the lunchroom.

Buttercup didn't even bother looking inside her lunchbox. She just tipped the contents straight into her mouth and gulped them down.

BUURRRPP!

"All done!" said Buttercup, wiping her mouth with the back of her hand. "NOW can we see Fat Mabel? PLEASE PLEASE PLEASE!"

"Not until everyone has finished eating," said Ms Keane.

Buttercup drummed her fingers impatiently on the lunch table. "Are you done?" she asked Bubbles.

Without waiting for a reply, Buttercup bolted down the other half of her sister's tuna sandwich. Then she gobbled up Blossom's apple.

"Hey!" said Blossom indignantly. "I was going to eat that."

When everyone had finally finished eating, Ms Keane said, "Now for the moment we've all been waiting for."

"Fat Mabel?" asked Buttercup hopefully.

"No," said Ms Keane. "The unveiling of the Rainbow Heart Tiara!"

Chatting excitedly, the children followed their teacher into a special gallery. They jostled each other to be first to catch a glimpse of the tiara.

"Me first!" said a tiny man in a black top hat and a monocle, shoving his way past.

"No pushing!" said Blossom. Then, noticing who it was, she said, "Oops! Sorry, Mayor. Didn't realise it was you."

"STOP!" A robot security guard rolled over to them. "No entry to the gallery without security clearance."

The shiny metal robot had infrared scanners and motion detectors. Red beams of light swept over each visitor as Robo-Guard scanned them.

As the robot's lasers swept over Buttercup, red lights flashed and an alarm blared.

BEEP! BEEP! BEEP!

"Weapon detected!" droned Robo-Guard,

pointing an X-ray gun at Buttercup's pocket.

"Oh, Buttercup," said Blossom, clapping a hand over her eyes in embarrassment.

"Aw!" Buttercup took a slingshot out of her pocket and reluctantly handed it to the robot.

Inside the gallery, there was a case covered by a silky black sheet. The Mayor of Townsville stood up to make a speech.

"Hello, boys and girls," said the Mayor, peering at them through his monocle. "Today is a very special day. And so, without further ado, I hereby unveil the er ... er ..."

"The Rainbow Heart Tiara," supplied Blossom.

"Oh yes," said the Mayor. "I hereby unveil the Rainbow Heart Tiara!"

He swept the sheet off the display case.

"Ooooooooohhhhh!" everyone gasped.

A gigantic red ruby shaped like a heart glittered in the middle of the gold tiara. On either side of the heart twinkled rows of sapphires, emeralds, pink diamonds and yellow topazes – a gorgeous rainbow of jewels.

"Wow!" breathed Blossom.

"It's so pretty!" cooed Bubbles.

"Whatever," said Buttercup, shrugging.

Bored, she leaned against the glass case.

"Security violation!" said Robo-Guard. "No touching!" The robot picked Buttercup up and moved her away from the case.

"Hey!" shouted Buttercup, kicking her legs. "Put me down!"

"According to legend," said Ms Keane, "the Rainbow Heart Tiara brings anyone who wears it bad luck. Cleopatra was wearing the tiara the night before she was bitten by a snake and died."

Blossom filled a whole notebook with notes as Ms Keane taught them about the tiara.

Finally, Ms Keane checked her watch and announced, "We need to get going."

"To see Fat Mabel?" Buttercup asked her teacher hopefully.

"No," said Ms Keane. "Back to school. Everyone back on the bus."

"This is so unfair," grumbled Buttercup as they headed towards the exit.

BEEP! BEEP! BEEP!!!

"What's that noise?" asked Bubbles.

"It's just another false alarm," said Buttercup. "Someone probably sneezed next to the tiara."

WHEE-OOO! WHEE-OOO! NORNK NORNK NORNK!

The alarm changed to an urgent wail, growing louder and louder.

"Uh-oh. That doesn't sound good," said Blossom, frowning.

"Something's really wrong!" shouted Bubbles.

Someone was trying to steal the Rainbow Heart Tiara!

SLEEPOVER AT THE MUSEUM

Can The Powerpuff Girls handle any more excitement after seeing the world's second-largest elastic-band ball?

The Powerpuff Girls flew back to the tiara gallery in a blaze of pink, blue and green light.

SWISH!

SWOOSH!

SWASH!

"INITIATING LOCKDOWN MODE!" bellowed Robo-Guard, rolling off to secure the museum's exits.

The Rainbow Heart Tiara was still twinkling in its glass display case.

"Phew!" panted Blossom. "The tiara's still here."

"Maybe it's a false alarm," said Bubbles.

"Let's split up and check the room," suggested Blossom. "We don't want to miss any clues."

"Good idea," said Buttercup. She peered at the display case. There were smudges on the glass. "That's strange," she said, taking a closer look. "These marks don't look like human fingerprints."

Blossom began searching for any clues.

She spotted a yellow thread on the floor. "Aha!" she cried. "The intruder is wearing something yellow."

Bubbles held up a hair. "And he has short, brown hair."

"Look!" Blossom shouted, pointing across the room.

A long, thin tail was sticking out of an air vent at the base of the wall. The Powerpuff Girls ran over but the tail quickly disappeared from view.

Bubbles knelt on the floor. "Mousie!" she called into the vent. "Oh, little mousie. Come out and play!"

"It's not a mouse," said Buttercup. "It's a rat."

"That's OK," said Bubbles. "Rats are cute, too!"

"Think about it, Bubbles," said Blossom. "The tiara is very shiny. That's not just any rat, it's—"

"Pack Rat!" gasped Bubbles.

"Got there in the end," muttered Buttercup, rolling her eyes.

Robo-Guard rushed back into the tiara gallery. "Lockdown complete." He herded The Powerpuff Girls out of the room. "Authorised personnel only. Return to the assembly point."

"You don't understand," said Blossom. "We can help."

"We're superheroes," explained Bubbles.

"We can catch the intruder," said Buttercup.

"Permission denied," said Robo-Guard, picking up The Powerpuff Girls and wheeling them back to the museum entrance. The Mayor, their classmates, a few puzzled-looking tourists and a tour guide were gathered there.

BANG! BANG! BANG!

Ms Keane was hammering her fists on the

steel shutters blocking the museum's doors. "Let us out!"

"Request denied," said Robo-Guard. "Nobody will leave the premises until the intruder has been apprehended."

"Are you telling me we could be here all night?" said Ms Keane, looking horrified.

"Woo hoo!" cheered the children. "Sleepover at the museum!"

Robo-Guard rolled off to patrol the museum, his red lasers flashing.

"This is going to be so cool!" said Bubbles. "I love sleepovers!"

"But I didn't pack a toothbrush," said Blossom.

"Finally!" said Buttercup. "Fat Mabel, here I come!"

But instead of taking them to see the

cannons, Ms Keane took the children to the science gallery. There were magnets and other fun science experiments to try.

"I'm hungry," said Buttercup. "What's for dinner? Are we supposed to gnaw on dinosaur bones?"

Ms Keane led the children into the museum café. "Help yourselves to anything," she said wearily.

"Yay!" cried the children, piling their trays high with crisps, sweets, pots of jelly, packs of chewing gum and cans of fizzy drink.

"Would anyone like a pickle?" asked the Mayor, passing around a big jar of pickles.

Buttercup guzzled a can of soda in one gulp and let out a loud belch. She crushed the metal can in one hand and threw it

across the room. It landed right in the recycling bin!

"Slam dunk!" she cheered, popping a wad of chewing gum in her mouth. "Can we go and see the cannon now?"

"No," said Ms Keane. "It's time for a nice, calm craft activity."

The children trotted into the museum's art room. There were crayons, coloured paper and glue set out on little tables.

"Tomorrow is Valentine's Day," said Ms Keane. "So you can all make a card for someone special."

Blossom looked at the supplies and shook her head. "Good thing I came prepared," she said, pulling a plastic case out of her backpack. She opened it up, revealing compartments filled with sequins, sticky tape

and stencils. There was even a handy pocket-sized staple gun!

In no time at all Blossom had made a beautiful heart-shaped card. It had a lacy border and sparkled with pink sequins.

"That's pretty," said Bubbles. "Who is it for?"

"I haven't decided yet," said Blossom. She shot a shy glance at Jared, who was busy colouring pink flowers on his card.

"Mine's for Donny the Unicorn," Bubbles said, sticking colourful sequins on her card's rainbow design.

Dear Donny, she wrote. *Happy Valentine's Day from your BFF.*

"Why aren't you making a card, Buttercup?" asked Blossom.

"Because it's stupid," grumbled Buttercup, crumpling up her sheet of paper. "Pack Rat is on the loose. We shouldn't be wasting time making things."

"Actually," said Blossom thoughtfully, "maybe that's exactly what we *should* be doing."

"OK," said Bubbles. "I'll make another Valentine for Professor Utonium."

"Not a card, Bubbles," said Blossom. "We should make a booby trap."

"Hee hee," laughed Buttercup.

"What's so funny?" asked Blossom.

"You said booby!" chuckled Buttercup.

"Buttercup!" Blossom shook her head at her sister.

The Powerpuff Girls sneaked out of the craft room and crept back to the café. They took all of the empty drinks cans out of the recycling bin and strung them together using Blossom's hair ribbon.

"Let's hang it across the entrance to the tiara room," said Buttercup. "It will rattle if anyone trips over it."

But as The Powerpuff Girls headed towards the tiara room, they bumped into Robo-Guard patrolling the corridor.

"Bedtime!" said the robot.

"But it's only seven o'clock," protested Bubbles.

"Growing girls need their sleep," answered the robot.

The museum was getting dark and a bit creepy. Dinosaur skeletons cast spooky

shadows on the walls and their footsteps echoed as Robo-Guard marched them into the great hall, where there was a temporary exhibit called "Sleeping Bags Through the Ages".

"That's a bit of luck," said Blossom.

Their classmates and the other visitors were getting ready for bed.

The Mayor shivered.

"Oh dear," he said nervously. "I'm afraid of the dark."

"Don't worry," Bubbles reassured the Mayor, patting his shoulder. "We'll protect you."

"As usual," muttered Buttercup.

"I bagsie this one," said Buttercup,

wriggling into a camouflage sleeping bag made of high-tech insulated material.

"This one's mine!" cried Blossom. She crawled into a pink silk sleeping bag said to have belonged to Marie Antoinette.

"Ooh! This looks cosy," said the Mayor. He took off his top hat and monocle and slipped inside a prehistoric fur-lined sleeping bag. A moment later he was snoring loudly.

"Where can I sleep?" said Bubbles, looking around. "There aren't any sleeping bags left."

"You can have that one," said Ms Keane, pointing to a pile of straw. It was labelled 'Medieval Peasant's Sleeping Bag'.

"I've definitely drawn the short straw," Bubbles said, lying down on the pile. She squirmed around, trying to get comfortable.

43

Blossom pulled out a notebook and flipped through the pages. "Rats are nocturnal creatures," she told her sisters, reading the notes she'd taken in the natural history section. "Pack Rat will probably try to come back at night."

"We'll be ready for him!" said Buttercup. "As soon as the others are asleep, we can sneak out and set the booby trap."

"I wish Octi was here," said Bubbles, picking straw out of her hair.

"Shhh!" Ms Keane said, putting a finger to her lips. "I'm going to read you a bedtime story. It's called *Fossils Are Fun*." She opened the book and started reading. "Billions of years ago, long before the dinosaurs, small furry creatures called fossils roamed the earth. Blah … blah … blah …"

One by one, The Powerpuff Girls'
classmates nodded off to sleep. Soon, even
Ms Keane was snoring.

ZZZZZZZZ!

Glancing over at her sisters, Buttercup
noticed that their eyes were starting to shut,
too. "Hey!" she whispered. "Don't fall asleep.
We've got a job to do!"

*Aren't you glad this story is more
exciting than* Fossils Are Fun?

TO CATCH A THIEF

The Powerpuff Girls were off to set a trap — a Pack Rat trap!

Blossom, Bubbles and Buttercup scrambled out of their sleeping bags and tiptoed past their sleeping classmates. They flew silently through the museum's silent

galleries and dark corridors. A sign pointed left to the military history room.

"Fat Mabel!" Buttercup started to turn left.

"No, Buttercup," said Blossom, pulling her sister back. "The tiara's this way."

"Oh, man," grumbled Buttercup as they turned right.

When they reached the room where the Rainbow Heart Tiara was on display, Blossom got out her mini staple gun. She stapled one end of the booby trap to the wall.

STAPLE!

Stretching the string of drinks cans across the doorway, she stapled the other end to the opposite side.

STAPLE!

The trip wire hung across the doorway,

just above the floor.

The Powerpuff Girls gazed at the Rainbow Heart Tiara. Moonlight streamed in through a skylight, making the tiara's jewels twinkle like the stars above.

"I wish I could try it on," sighed Bubbles.

"Not a good idea," said Blossom. "It's supposed to bring bad luck."

"But it's so pretty …" said Bubbles longingly.

"Step away from the tiara," ordered Buttercup.

Bubbles took a step backwards.

CRASH! RATTLE!

She had set off the booby trap!

"Oopsie!" said Bubbles.

"I guess we didn't even need to try it on to have bad luck," said Blossom.

Suddenly, red light blazed into the room.

"Intruders detected," said Robo-Guard, his lasers sweeping over The Powerpuff Girls. He grabbed Blossom, Bubbles and Buttercup in one huge metallic fist and wheeled them to the great hall.

"Back to bed!" blared the robot. "It is a scientific fact that growing girls need plenty of rest."

"Robo-Guard's voice sounds really familiar," said Blossom.

"Yeah," said Bubbles. "I just can't place it."

"Nighty night. Sleep tight," said the robot, tucking Blossom, Bubbles and Buttercup into their sleeping bags.

"Maybe he sounds like someone on TV," said Buttercup.

As soon as Robo-Guard was out of sight, The Powerpuff Girls got out of their sleeping bags again. They tiptoed out of the room and – **BUMP!** – crashed right into Robo-Guard!

"Movement detected," barked Robo-Guard.

"Er, I just needed the toilet," said Blossom.

Robo-Guard escorted them to the bathroom and waited outside. He took them

back to their sleeping bags then headed off on patrol.

"This is impossible," said Blossom. "Robo-Guard won't let us help. And his motion sensors can tell whenever we get out of bed."

"If you want to catch a rat, you need to act like a rat," said Buttercup.

Bubbles stuck her front teeth out and said, "Squeak! Squeak!"

"No," said Buttercup. "I mean that the only way to get around the museum without Robo-Guard stopping us is through the air vents – like Pack Rat."

The Powerpuff Girls ran to the display of Townsville's earliest tools. Blossom used her laser vision to cut through the glass display case. Grabbing Ye Olde Cordless Drill, Buttercup quickly unscrewed the metal plate

covering the nearest air vent. One by one, they wriggled in.

"Pew-yew," said Bubbles, behind her. "Your feet stink, Buttercup."

"Ew," said Blossom. "It's so dusty in here!"

As they crawled along on their bellies, Blossom said, "We need some bait for our trap."

"There's probably some cheese in the café," said Bubbles.

"This is Pack Rat we're talking about," said Blossom. "We don't need cheese. We need—"

"Shiny things!" said Buttercup.

"Then it's a good thing I remembered to accessorise," said Bubbles.

It was pitch black in the tunnels but luckily Blossom had copied the museum map

into one of her notebooks. She knew exactly where to go.

"We're over the dinosaur room now," she whispered.

The Powerpuff Girls lifted off a ceiling panel and looked down at the room full of dinosaur skeletons.

Buttercup spat out a huge wad of bubblegum. She stuck it to the ceiling.

"Gross," said Blossom. "Put it in a bin."

Ignoring her sister, Buttercup held on to the gum and jumped down. The gum stretched like an elastic band.

BOING!

Hovering just above the floor, Buttercup rigged up a trap using stegosaurus bones.

"Chuck down some bait, Bubbs," she whispered.

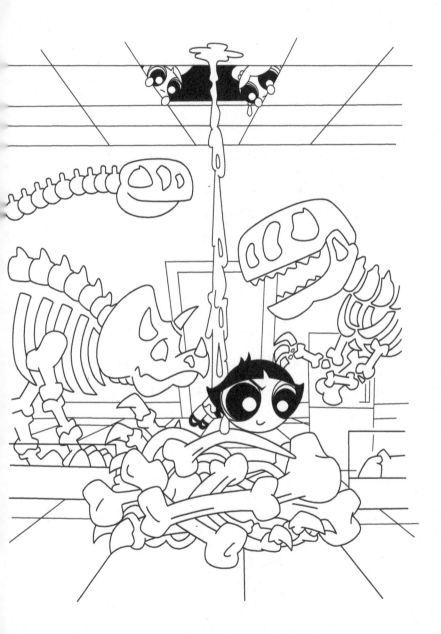

Bubbles threw down her glittery necklace. Buttercup put it in the middle of the trap.

"Reel me in," hissed Buttercup.

Bubbles and Blossom started pulling up the chewing gum.

"Yuck! This is so unhygienic," said Blossom.

"Hurry!" hissed Buttercup. "Robo-Guard is coming!"

Buttercup's sisters pulled her up just in time. Blossom slid the ceiling panel back in place just as the robot marched into the room.

The Powerpuff Girls slithered along the ceiling until they reached the rocks and minerals room.

"I'll go this time," said Blossom.

Buttercup offered her the wad of gum.

"No, thanks," said Blossom, pulling a face. "I'll fly."

"Oh, yeah," said Buttercup. "Why didn't I think of that?"

Lifting off the ceiling panel, Blossom flew down to the gallery.

Bubbles threw down two bracelets.

Blossom put a glittery bracelet on the ground. **SNAP!** She broke the string of the other bracelet.

"Hey!" said Bubbles. "That was my favourite one."

"Sorry, Bubbs," said Blossom. "I had to."

Blossom scattered the beads over the floor. If anyone tried to get the glittery bait,

they'd slip on the beads.

Blossom flew back up to her sisters. They went to every gallery, setting snares and booby traps in each one. Finally, they came to the military history room.

Blossom lifted off the ceiling panel. The Powerpuff Girls looked down.

An enormous cannon was right below them. It had massive wheels and a shiny muzzle. A pyramid of huge cannonballs was piled up next to it.

"Oh, man," breathed Buttercup, staring at Fat Mabel in awe. "She's even more beautiful than I'd imagined."

Buttercup flew down and sat on the cannon, resting her cheek against the enormous weapon. "150 tons of pure firepower," she said, stroking Fat Mabel.

SQUEAK! SQUEAK! SQUEAK!

The sound of a wheel came down the hallway. Robo-Guard was on patrol!

"Hurry up, Buttercup," Blossom called down. "You need to get out of there."

The footsteps were getting closer and closer, but Buttercup hadn't budged.

"OK, we're going in," said Bubbles. She and Blossom swooped down.

"Move!" ordered Blossom. "Or we're going to get caught."

"No!" wailed Buttercup, clinging on to the cannon. "You'll never come between me and Fat Mabel!"

Blossom and Bubbles used their super-strength to pry Buttercup off the cannon. They flew their sister back up to the ceiling just as the robot entered the room.

"Phew!" said Blossom, panting. "That was a close call."

"So?" Bubbles asked her sister. "Did you like Fat Mabel?"

Buttercup nodded dreamily. "She really blew me away."

"I hate to drag you away," said Blossom,

"but we should probably try to get some sleep."

The Powerpuff Girls crawled through the air vents back to the great hall.

Blossom yawned and snuggled into her pink sleeping bag. "I'm so tired."

"Me too," said Buttercup. She shut her eyes, already dreaming of Fat Mabel.

Bubbles burrowed into her pile of straw. Prickly straws snapped underneath her as she wriggled around, trying to get comfy.

Suddenly, she heard a much louder sound.

CRUNCH!

"Did you hear that?" asked Bubbles, sitting up.

"It must be one of the traps!" said Blossom.

"Maybe we caught Pack Rat!" said Buttercup.

Well, what are we waiting for – let's go and find out!

THE MAYOR GETS IN A PICKLE

> *Did Pack Rat take the glittery bait? Or is someone else up past their bedtime?*

The Powerpuff Girls shot out of the great hall. Strange noises were coming from down the hall.

CRUNCH!

MUNCH!

"The sound's coming from down there," said Blossom, pointing to a small gallery off to the side.

"But there's nothing in there except a display of antique pickle jars," said Bubbles.

They flew to the room and saw a small figure in a top hat, surrounded by pickle jars. A strong smell of vinegar filled the room.

"Er, hello, girls," said the Mayor. "I seem  to have got myself in a sticky situation." He tried to lift up his feet, but his shoes were stuck to the ground with a huge wads of chewing gum.

"Good to see that my patented Bubblegum Booby Trap worked," said Buttercup.

"Why are you up?" asked Blossom.

"I wanted a midnight snack," explained the Mayor, munching a bumpy green pickle.

"Aren't those hundreds of years old?" asked Blossom, looking a bit queasy.

"That's the wonderful thing about pickles," said the Mayor. "They get even better with age." He offered the girls a mouldy pickle jar.

"Er, no thanks," said Blossom.

"I'm full," said Bubbles, shaking her head.

Even Buttercup couldn't be tempted!

Using their super-strength, The Powerpuff Girls pulled the Mayor by his arms. The chewing gum stretched and stretched and stretched until – **SNAP!** – the Mayor and The Powerpuff Girls shot across the room and crashed into the pickle jars.

SMASH!

Ancient pickle jars shattered around them. Pickle juice puddled on the floor.

Robo-Guard rolled into the room, red lasers flashing. "Access denied!" the robot boomed. He picked the tiny Mayor up in one hand and all three Powerpuff Girls in the other.

"The mayor just wanted a snack," Blossom tried to explain.

"Remember to brush your teeth before bed," droned the robot.

"I can't figure out who he reminds me of," said Buttercup as Robo-Guard marched them back to their classmates. "It's driving me crazy."

"I'll tell you what's driving me crazy," said Blossom. "Robo-Guard! He keeps messing

up our plans to stop Pack Rat!"

Despite all the commotion, Ms Keane and the rest of the class were still sound asleep.

"Anyone want to trade sleeping bags?" asked Bubbles hopefully. "You guys really shouldn't miss out on this unique historical experience."

"Nice try, Bubbs," said Buttercup, snuggling into her comfy sleeping bag.

Bubbles flopped down on her pile of straw. A mouse squeaked indignantly and ran across her chest.

"This is the last straw," said Bubbles.

"Oh dear," the Mayor said. "I can't get back to sleep."

"I'll sing you a lullaby," Bubbles offered. In her sweet voice she crooned:

Rockabye Mayor on the hard floor,

Just close your eyes and you'll start to snore.

Count lovely pickles so you fall asleep,

And dream until morning without a peep!

Soon the Mayor was sound asleep.

"Night, Blossom. Night, Buttercup," said Bubbles.

Her sisters didn't reply because the lullaby had sent them to sleep, too.

WHOOOOOOOA!

THUD!

"A superhero's work is never done," sighed Bubbles. She shook her sisters awake.

"Go away!" mumbled Buttercup. "I'm just about to fire Fat Mabel."

"Another trap's gone off," said Bubbles.

"It's probably just the Mayor again," said Blossom sleepily.

But the Mayor was still snoring in his

fur-lined sleeping bag.

"I'll dump a bucket of cold water over you
if you don't get up right now!" threatened
Bubbles.

Blossom and
Buttercup jumped out
of their sleeping bags.

"It sounded like it was
coming from down
there," said Bubbles,
pointing down the hall.

The Powerpuff Girls
hurried into the rocks and minerals gallery.

"Gotcha!" said Blossom, flying into the
room in a blaze of pink light.

But instead of Pack Rat, a dark-haired boy
with glasses was sprawled on the ground,
surrounded by beads.

Blossom gasped. "What are you doing in here, Jared?"

Jared thrust a crumpled Valentine's card with pink flowers on it at Blossom. "I sneaked out of bed to deliver your Valentine. But I got

lost in the dark and slipped."

Blossom helped Jared up. "Thanks," she said. "It's beautiful."

Buttercup made gagging noises. "Pass me a sick bag," she

grumbled. "I can't believe I interrupted my dream for this."

"This area is off-limits," Robo-Guard blared, barging into the room.

"Not you again," groaned Blossom.

"You should be trying to catch Pack Rat," said Bubbles. "Not us."

The guard robot scooped The Powerpuff Girls up in one hand. He grabbed Jared with the other hand. He deposited them all back in the great hall.

"We've got to do something about Robo-Guard," whispered Buttercup once they were back in their sleeping bags.

"What do you mean?" asked Blossom.

"That big hunk of metal keeps getting in the way," explained Buttercup. "We'll never catch Pack Rat at this rate."

"I've got a plan!" said Blossom. "But it might be dangerous."

"Danger?" said Buttercup, grinning. "That's my middle name."

"Come on!" Blossom led her sisters back

to the science display. "Help me stick all these magnets together," she said.

The Powerpuff Girls joined up all the magnets.

"Now we need to lure Robo-Guard in here," said Blossom.

"I'm on it," said Bubbles. She tried to fly away but she couldn't move. Her metal bracelet was stuck fast to the magnet!

"Ugghh!" she grunted. Bubbles wriggled her wrist out of the bracelet and flew into the hallway. "I'm going to steal the Rainbow Heart Tiara!" she sang loudly.

A moment later, Robo-Guard wheeled down the hallway. "Red alert!" he announced.

"Yoo hoo!" cried Bubbles. "Robo! In here!" She flew back into the science gallery

with Robo-Guard in hot pursuit.

THUNK!

The powerful magnetic force pulled the metal robot in. Robo-Guard struggled to break free but the magnets were too strong.

"You're grounded!" said the robot.

"No – you are!" Buttercup shot back.

"There," said Blossom, brushing her hands together. "That should keep him out of our way."

Bubbles yawned. "Maybe we can get a little sleep now—"

RATTLE! CLATTER!

From down the hall came the sound of rattling cans.

"That's the trip wire!" exclaimed Bubbles.

"Someone's really trying to steal the tiara this time!" gasped Blossom.

The Powerpuff Girls zipped down the hallway, leaving pink, blue and green trails behind them.

A rodent in a yellow jacket was holding the Rainbow Heart Tiara. It was Pack Rat!

ROBO-GUARD GOES ROGUE

> *Did you know that rats can survive being flushed down the toilet? They can fall five storeys without getting hurt. They can even survive nuclear radiation! So The Powerpuff Girls have their work cut out for them ...*

Pack Rat stroked the tiara adoringly. "My shiny!" he cooed. "I will bring you home to Baby Rita!"

"Drop it right now, you dirty rat!" yelled Buttercup.

Clutching the tiara, Pack Rat scurried towards the air vent.

"Not so fast," said Blossom, blocking the way. Pack Rat turned and fled. He jumped over the trip wire and sprinted down the corridor.

"After him!" shouted Buttercup.

The Powerpuff Girls flew down the hall.

"He's in here!" cried Bubbles, pointing to a room with a display of old coins.

Pack Rat was staring at the coins, mesmerised. "Shiny!" he said.

"Get him!" yelled Buttercup.

Blossom lunged to get Pack Rat, but he slipped out of her grasp and took off again.

"He's heading for the gift shop!" cried Blossom.

The Powerpuff Girls chased Pack Rat past yo-yos, bouncy balls, rubbers shaped like dinosaurs and giant pencils that said *Townsville Museum* on them.

"Ooh!" said Bubbles, distracted by a shelf full of cuddly toys. "Those are so cute!"

"Focus, Bubbles!" shouted Buttercup. "We can't let him get away!"

Pack Rat had stopped by a spinner of key chains. "Shiny!" he said, shoving them in his jacket pockets.

Buttercup grabbed the Rainbow Heart Tiara and tried to yank it away from Pack Rat.

"MY Shiny!" he yelled. He gave a desperate tug and the tiara slipped out of Buttercup's grasp. She crashed into a bookcase. A copy of *Fossils Are Fun* hit her on the head.

CLONK!

"Ouch!" said Buttercup. "That book really does my head in."

"Are you OK?" Blossom and Bubbles asked, helping her up.

"I'm fine!" said Buttercup, rubbing her head. "But Pack Rat won't be when I get my hands on him!"

The girls ran out of the gift shop. They saw Pack Rat's tail disappearing into the natural history gallery.

"Don't let him get away!" hollered Blossom, charging after him.

The stuffed animals looked creepier than ever in the dark, their glass eyes gleaming eerily in the moonlight. But there was no sign of Pack Rat.

"Where could he have gone?" said Blossom, looking around the exhibit.

"Oh, look," said Bubbles. "That little mousie is wearing a cute yellow jacket."

Pack Rat was standing perfectly still, trying to blend in with the other rodents.

"Hi-yah!" Buttercup yelled. She aimed a karate kick at Pack Rat, but hit a stuffed squirrel instead.

"Wrong rodent!" she said.

Pack Rat scuttled out of the gallery, clutching the tiara.

Blossom, Bubbles and Buttercup huddled behind the huge stuffed chinchillasaurus.

"This is ridiculous," said Buttercup. "That rotten rodent is running rings around us."

"I've got an idea," said Blossom. She whispered the plan to her sisters.

"I don't know," said Buttercup, frowning. "Isn't that just a legend? Does the tiara really bring bad luck?"

"It's worth a try," said Bubbles.

The Powerpuff Girls walked down the museum's main corridor.

"Pack Rat," Blossom sang. "We give up!"

"You can keep the tiara," called Buttercup.

Pack Rat peeked out of the pickle room.

"Go ahead," urged Bubbles. "Why don't you try it on?"

"I'm sure it will look great on you," flattered Blossom.

Grinning triumphantly, Pack Rat put the tiara on his head. "So shiny!" he said ecstatically.

"Bad move, dude," said Buttercup. "Your luck's just run out."

There was the sound of a wheel coming down the hallway. Robo-Guard had escaped!

The Powerpuff Girls pressed themselves against the wall as he thundered past. "INTRUDER DETECTED!" the robot bellowed.

He picked Pack Rat up by the scruff of his neck. The tiara flew off Pack Rat's head and

sailed across the room. Buttercup leapt up
and caught it like a Frisbee.

"ALERT! ALERT! UNAUTHORISED
ACTIVITY!" Robo-Guard blared, dropping
Pack Rat to the floor.

"No!" cried Bubbles. "Don't let him get
away!"

Pack Rat scuttled into a nearby bathroom
and disappeared.

"Oh, man!" muttered Buttercup. "All that work down the drain."

"Literally," said Blossom.

CRASH!

Robo-Guard picked up an ancient pickle jar and threw it at the floor.

"Whoa, dude!" said Buttercup. "I thought you didn't like people touching the exhibits!"

Robo-Guard marched into the next gallery. He smashed a display case, shattering the glass. He flung prehistoric tin openers around the room.

"TIDY UP TIME!" bellowed the robot.

"What's wrong with him?" said Bubbles. "He's acting really weird."

"The magnets must have messed up his programming!" said Blossom.

"He's gone rogue!" yelled Buttercup.

Robo-Guard wheeled into the dinosaur hall. He kicked over a T-Rex skeleton. Big bones landed on the floor in a jumble.

"Stop that!" shouted Blossom. "You're destroying the museum!" She picked up a bone and swung it at the robot. He batted it away with his right fist.

Buttercup charged at Robo-Guard, wielding a T-Rex tooth like a dagger. Robo-Guard swatted it away with his left fist.

"REMEMBER TO BRUSH YOUR TEETH!" bellowed the robot.

Robo-Guard rolled into the rocks and minerals gallery.

Rocks tumbled to the floor as the robot smashed display cabinets with his fists. Blossom, Bubbles and Buttercup picked

them up and pelted Robo-Guard.

PING! PING! PING! The rocks bounced off his metal body, not even denting it.

"GO BACK TO BED! GROWING GIRLS NEED THEIR SLEEP!" the robot bellowed. He picked up the enormous meteorite from Mars and flung it at The Powerpuff Girls.

CRASH!

The Powerpuff Girls ducked just in time, but the meteorite smashed a cabinet full of fossils.

The robot wheeled off down the hall.

"WAKEY, WAKEY!" bellowed the robot. "TIME TO GET UP FOR SCHOOL!"

"He's heading into the sleeping bag room!" gasped Blossom.

"We can't let him hurt our classmates!" cried Bubbles.

Using all of her superstrength, Buttercup picked up the world's second largest ball of rubber bands. She rolled it down the corridor like a bowling ball.

POW! It hit Robo-Guard and knocked him over.

"Yay!" cheered Buttercup. "Strike!"

But Robo-Guard got straight back up. "MIND YOUR MANNERS!" he blared. "THAT IS NO WAY TO TREAT A GROWN-UP!" He charged at The Powerpuff Girls.

"Uh oh. There's only one woman who can help us now!" said Buttercup.

"I don't think Ms Keane will be much use against Robo-Guard," said Blossom.

"Not Ms Keane!" said Buttercup. "Fat Mabel!"

The Powerpuff Girls flew to the cannon room. Robo-Guard sped after them.

"Ammunition!" shouted Buttercup.

Blossom and Bubbles tossed her cannonballs. Buttercup loaded them into the cannon. "I've been dying to do this all day," she said excitedly.

Green lasers shot out of Buttercup's eyes.
The cannonball got hotter and hotter until it
finally caught light.

"IT'S NOT SAFE TO PLAY WITH FIRE!"
bellowed Robo-Guard.

"Get ready to become scrap metal!"
shouted Buttercup.

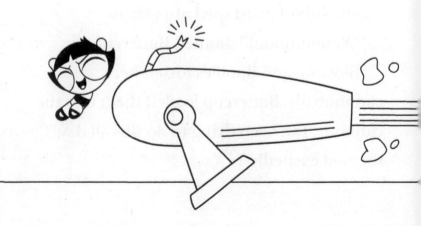

KA-BOOM!

A cannonball blasted out of Fat Mabel.
Chunks of metal rained down as the cannon
smashed Robo-Guard to smithereens.

"Yay!" cheered Blossom.

"Way to go, Buttercup!" said Bubbles.

"It wasn't me," said Buttercup. She threw

her arms around the still-smoking cannon
and gave it a big hug. "I love you, Fat Mabel!"

Aw! That Buttercup is such a softie! (But don't tell her I said that!)

VALENTINE'S DAY

> *Ah! Love is in the air! Or maybe that's just Buttercup's cheesy feet ...*

The sun was just beginning to rise over Townsville. As pale dawn light streamed through the museum's windows, The Powerpuff Girls stared at the wreckage from

the night's battle. Shards of glass from broken display cases lay shattered on the floor. Precious artefacts were strewn everywhere.

Buttercup yawned. "Maybe we can get a little rest before the other kids wake up."

"No way," said Blossom. "We need to get this mess cleared up!"

She rolled up her sleeves and concentrated hard. Pink light shot out of Blossom's eyes and hovered in the air. It took the shape of a broom. Her pink broom aura started to sweep up broken glass.

SWEEP! SWEEP! SWEEP!

Soon, every single shard of glass had been tidied up.

Blossom, Bubbles and Buttercup zipped around the museum, putting things back

where they belonged.

Blossom dusted off the displays of old tools and rearranged the antique pickle jars. She hid the empty ones the Mayor had snacked on at the back.

Bubbles cleaned up the animal exhibit. "There you go," she said, picking up a stuffed squirrel and putting it back into position.

"I'm too tired for heavy lifting," said Buttercup, yawning.

She narrowed her eyes and green light shot out. Her bulldozer aura glowed in the air.

VROOM!

The bulldozer scooped up the world's second-largest rubber band ball and put it back on display.

VROOM!

It lifted the meteorite from Mars back on to its pedestal.

Next, The Powerpuff Girls went into the dinosaur hall. A pile of T-Rex bones lay jumbled on the floor.

"I think this one goes here," said Blossom.

"And these thingies sort of fit together," said Buttercup.

"This might be the tail," said Bubbles.

They stepped back and looked at their work. "Hmm," said Blossom, frowning. "That doesn't look quite right."

The T-Rex skeleton had six legs and two tails.

"We need Rexy's help," said Bubbles. Blue light shone out of her eyes. Her T-Rex aura floated in the air.

Copying Bubbles's dino aura, the girls

quickly rearranged the bones into a T-Rex shape.

Last of all, The Powerpuff Girls brought the Rainbow Heart Tiara back to its special room.

Bubbles stared at the tiara, glittering in the morning sunshine. "It couldn't hurt if I tried it on for just one second ..."

She reached out her hand but Buttercup karate-chopped it away.

"Ouchie!" cried Bubbles.

"Remember what happened to Pack Rat?" Blossom reminded her sternly.

"Don't remind me," groaned Buttercup. "I can't believe he got away."

"Are we done now?" asked Bubbles, rubbing her eyes. "I'm soooo tired."

"Not yet," said Buttercup. "We still need to clean up the cannon room. It's full of bits of Robo-Guard."

But when they reached Fat Mabel's room, the chunks of metal had all been tidied up. Every trace of Robo-Guard had disappeared.

"That's strange," said Blossom.

"Goodbye, Fat Mabel!" said Buttercup, planting a big kiss on the cannon. "I'll never forget you!"

"Are you crying, Buttercup?" asked Bubbles.

"No!" snapped Buttercup, hastily wiping away a tear. "I've got something in my eye."

When they got back to the sleeping bag gallery, The Powerpuff Girls' classmates were

just waking up.

"Good morning," Blossom said to Jared. "Did you sleep well?"

"I had the weirdest dream," said Jared, stretching. "There was a big rat running around the museum."

"Sounds like a real nightmare," said Blossom.

The Mayor passed around a jar of ancient pickles. "Breakfast, anyone?"

Once everyone had rolled up their sleeping bags (and Bubbles had swept up her pile of straw), Ms Keane announced, "Time to go!"

"Aw!" complained one of the boys. "But we never got to visit the gift shop!"

"Trust me," said Buttercup, rubbing the lump *Fossils Are Fun* had left on her head,

"you don't want to go there."

The Powerpuff Girls slumped in the back row of the school bus and snoozed all the way home.

"How was the school trip, girls?" asked Professor Utonium as they staggered wearily through the front door.

"It was a blast," said Buttercup. "Literally."

"You must be hungry," said the Professor. "I've made breakfast."

There were envelopes addressed to each of the girls on the table.

"Maybe it's a letter from the president," said Blossom.

"I sent him some suggestions for ending climate change."

But it wasn't from the White House. It was a card with candy on the front that said, "You're the sweetest!"

"I wonder if mine is a letter from Donny the Unicorn," said Bubbles. She opened a card with a picture two fuzzy bumblebees and a message that read, "Bee Mine!"

"I bet Chas from Sensitive Thugz finally replied to my fan letter," said Buttercup, tearing open her envelope in hopes of finding a message from her favourite pop singer. Inside was a card with a picture of a digger. The message said, "I really dig you!"

"Happy Valentine's Day, girls!" Professor Utonium said. He served them plates of heart-shaped pancakes topped with

strawberries and whipped cream.

"Thanks for our Valentine's cards, Professor," said Blossom.

"We love you!" said Bubbles, giving Professor Utonium a hug.

"And we love these pancakes!" mumbled Buttercup, shovelling a huge bite into her mouth.

"Don't talk with your mouth full, young lady," said Professor Utonium sternly.

Blossom gasped. "I've just realised who Robo-Guard reminded me of!"

"Professor Utonium!" all three Powerpuff Girls cried together.

"Well that's hardly surprising," said Professor Utonium, smiling. "I invented Robo-Guard, after all. How's he doing?"

"Er ..." said Buttercup.

Deep underneath the Townsville dump, someone else was getting a Valentine's Day surprise ...

"Shiny things for Baby Rita!" crooned Pack Rat. He lovingly laid gleaming pieces of metal in front of the plastic doll.

Now Robo-Guard – or what was left of him – was on display in Pack Rat's cave!

101

Back at The Powerpuff Girls' house, Blossom, Bubbles and Buttercup had each polished off a second helping of pancakes.

"Oh no," said Blossom. "We forgot to bring home the Valentine's cards we made at the museum."

"That's OK," said Buttercup. "I know who my heart belongs to."

"Fat Mabel?" guessed Bubbles.

"Nope," said Buttercup. "The two of you!"

"Aw!" Blossom said, beaming. "Right back at you, sis!"

"Happy Valentine's Day!" said Bubbles, hugging her sisters tight. "I love you guys!"

And we love The Powerpuff Girls too!

THE END

CALLING ALL PPG FANS!

What's Mojo Jojo's deepest secret?
Which villains are in a book club?
And which episode features a dancing panda?

Dazzle your friends with facts about
The Powerpuff Girls, play quizzes and games and find
out secret information about all your favourite characters in:

THE POWERPUFF GIRLS OFFICIAL HANDBOOK!